Dedicated to Dr. Willie Tolliver,
who taught me how to talk about race.

This is Chase.
Chase is a black race car.

This is Ace.
Ace is a white race car.

They live in a world with lots of other race cars.
Big ones, small ones, short ones, tall ones,
old ones, new ones, black ones, blue ones,
pink ones, white ones,
wrong ones and right ones.

Chase and Ace have been best friends forever.
For as long as they can remember they have been training
together for the world famous, annual race car race. Last
year, they were finally old enough to enter the race.

For as long as anyone could remember, every year when the big race came around, a white car would win the race. A white car would win 4th place, third place, second place and the most important of all, first place. Until last year...

Last year Chase won the race. Last year Chase won first place. Ace won fourth place. Sometimes competition can come between friends, but not for these two. Ace was so happy for Chase, and Chase was so happy for Ace. They loved to race and did not care about place.

There were however, some cars that did care about place. These cars were on the race committee. No one had ever seen them, but everyone knew who they were. They held all the power in the world and made all the rules for the annual race car race. Rumor has it - the members of the race committee were all white cars.

When the committee heard about Chase winning, they were not happy. As long as the white cars kept winning the race, the members could keep their space on the committee. If other cars started to win, who knows what would happen?
They were worried.

"How could this have happened?" they roared!

"White cars have the fastest tires and the most powerful engines! How could a black car have won first place?
This is a disgrace!"

The committee decided to change a few rules to make it easier for the white cars to win and harder for all the other cars to win.

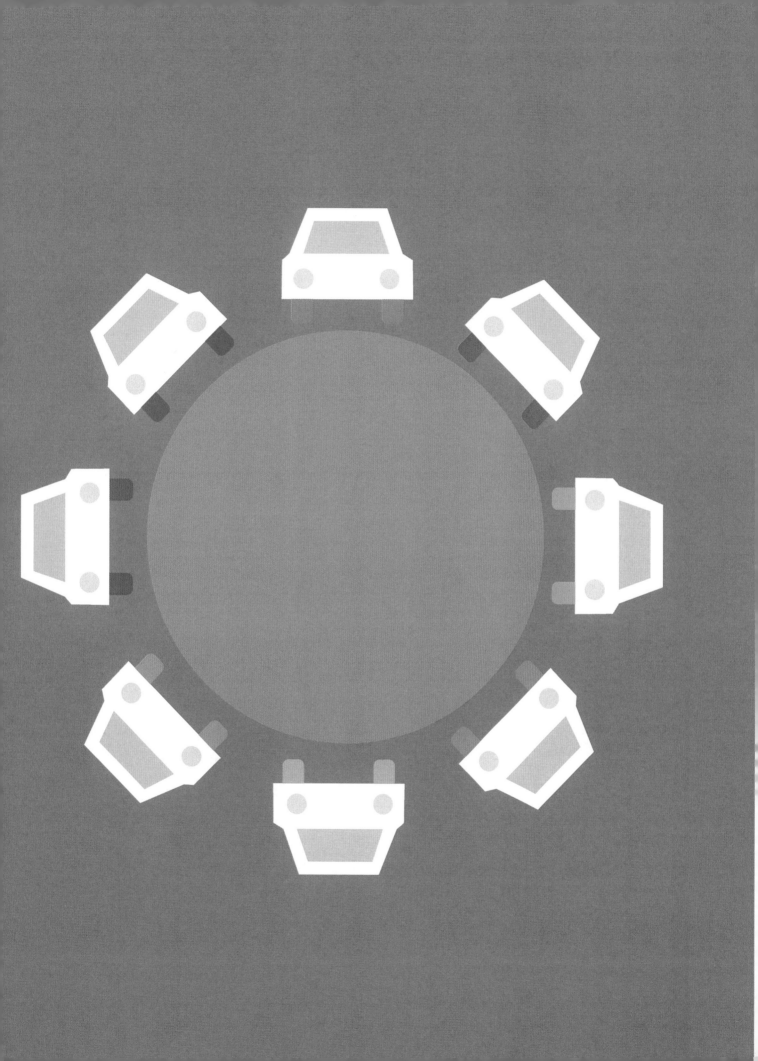

Next year rolled around and Chase and Ace were ready to race again. They had spent all summer training and knew the route by heart.

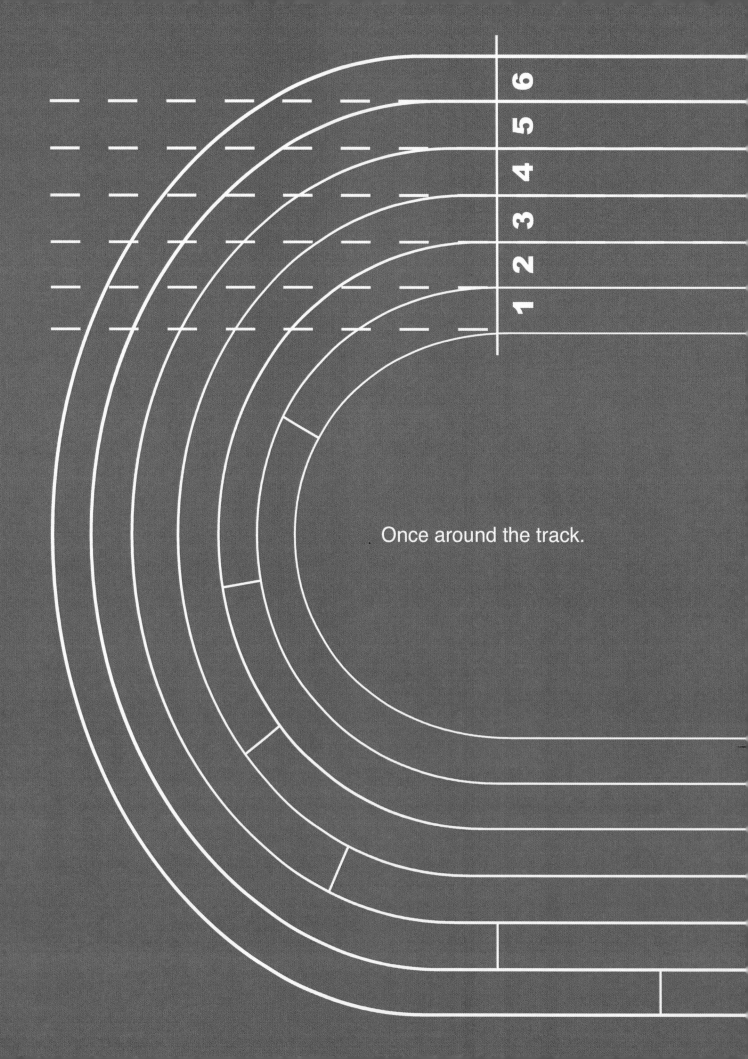

Once around the track.

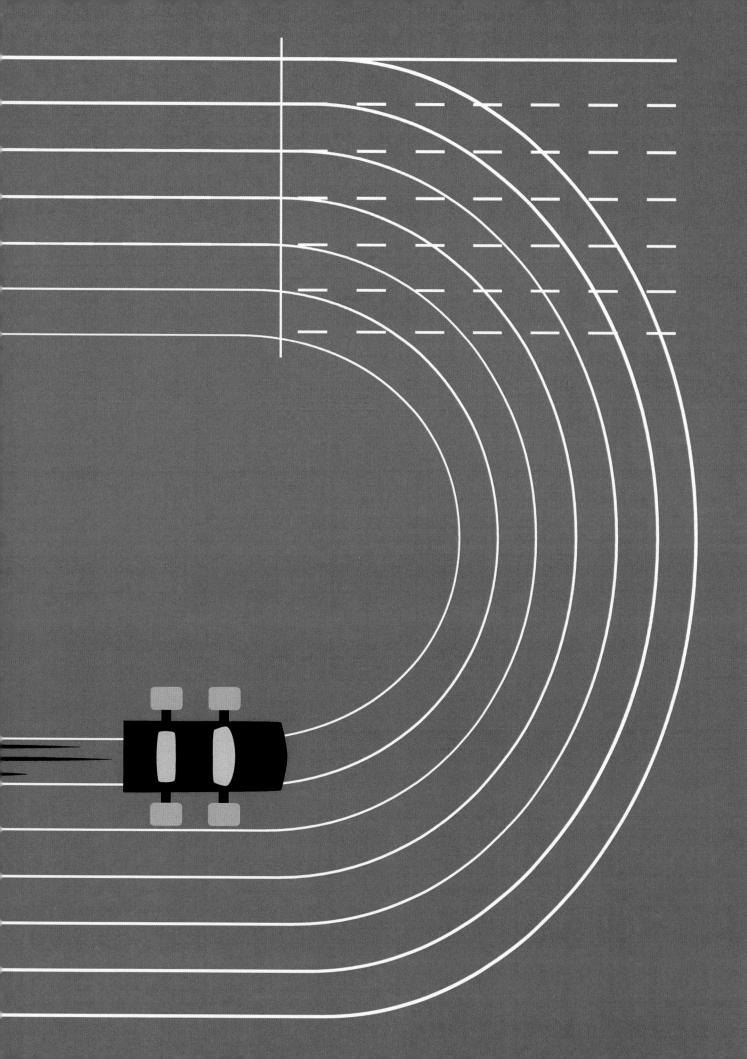

Straight through the cornfield.

Over blue mountain.

Through the magical forest.

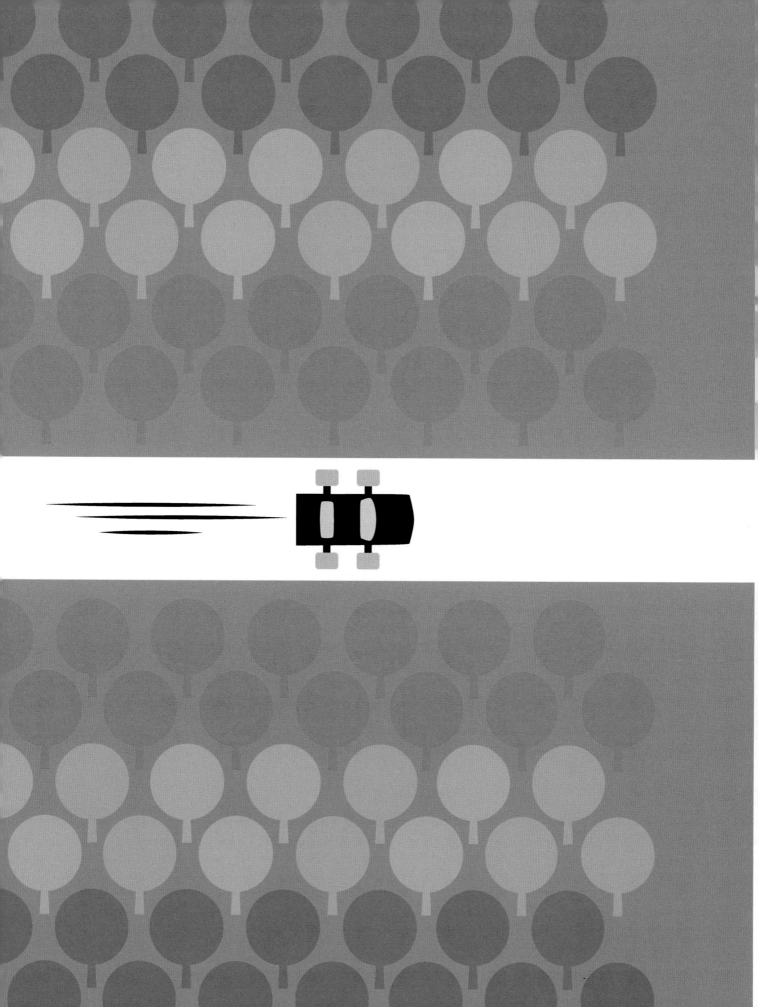

Across the bridge and over the finish line.

Race day had come. Chase started off faster than ever.

He zipped around the track as the crowds cheered him on.

Then he shot through the cornfields in record time.

He made it up blue mountain in the blink of an eye.

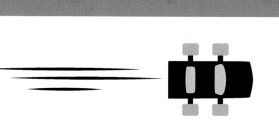

He wove through the trees in the magical forest.

Chase was getting ready to cross the bridge when he noticed a sign that had not been there before.

"Bridge is for white cars only. All other cars must go around the river". Chase paused for a second, *"Hmm...that's strange"* he thought, but he did not want to waste any more time. Chase sped around the river as fast as he could and jumped over the finish line.

Even without taking the bridge, Chase managed to come in second place. Ace came in third place. Ace was so happy for Chase, and Chase was so happy for Ace. They loved to race and did not care about place.

Bridge is
for white
cars only

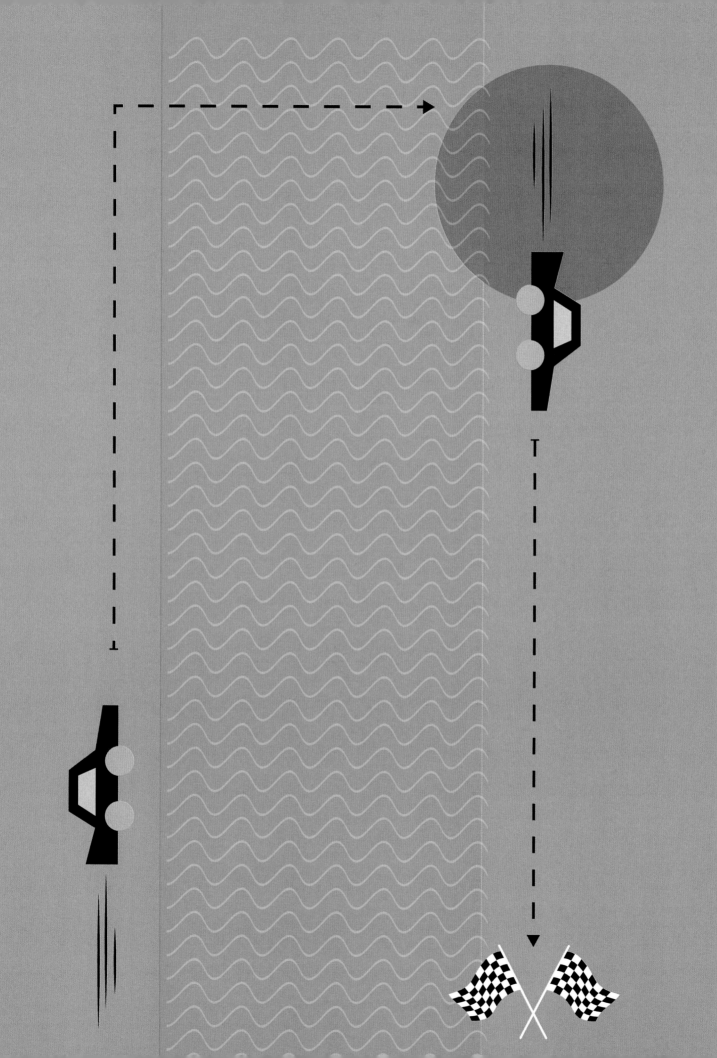

But back at home, something was bothering Chase. It just did not seem fair that the bridge was for whites only - it took twice as long to go around the river! He reminded himself that he just loved racing and that it didn't really matter whether he won or not. But he could not help feeling like he was not as good as the other cars - was something wrong with him? He shrugged it off and decided to train even harder for next year.

Back at Ace's house, Ace was snuggled up in bed smiling. He loved to race and did not care about place, but boy oh boy did it feel good to win a bronze medal this year! He drifted off to sleep dreaming of next year's race car race.

When the committee heard about Chase winning second place, they were not happy. *"How could a black car have won second place?! This is a disgrace!"* The committee decided to change a few more rules to make it easier for the white cars to win and harder for all other cars to win.

START

He zipped around the track as the crowds cheered him on.

The next year rolled around and Chase and Ace were ready to race.

Chase started off faster than ever.

He made it up blue mountain in the blink of an eye.

Then he shot through the cornfields in record time.

Chase was heading for the magical forest when he noticed something he had never seen before, a forked road with a new sign. *"Whites stay to the left and all other cars stay to the right."* Chase paused for a second, *"Hmm…that's strange"* he thought, but he did not want to waste any more time.

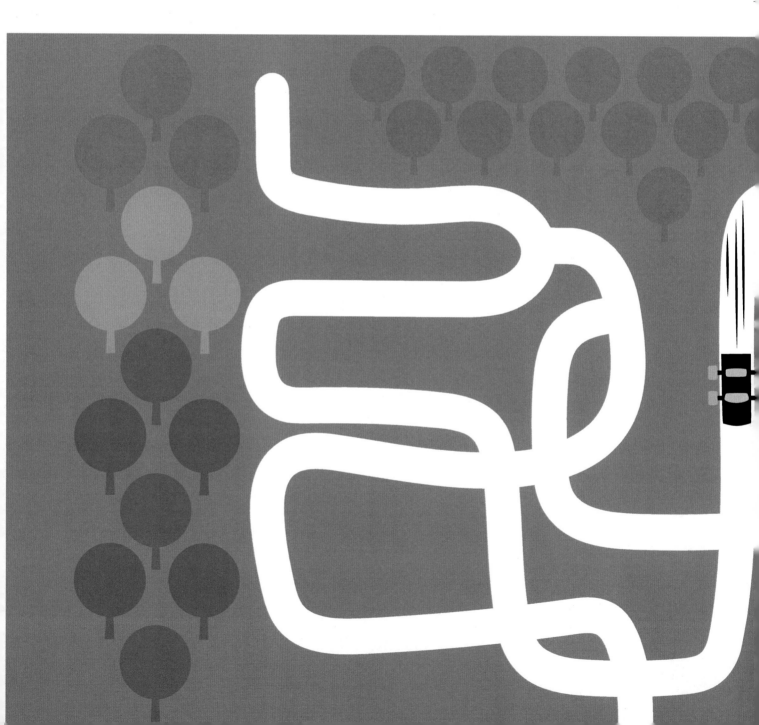

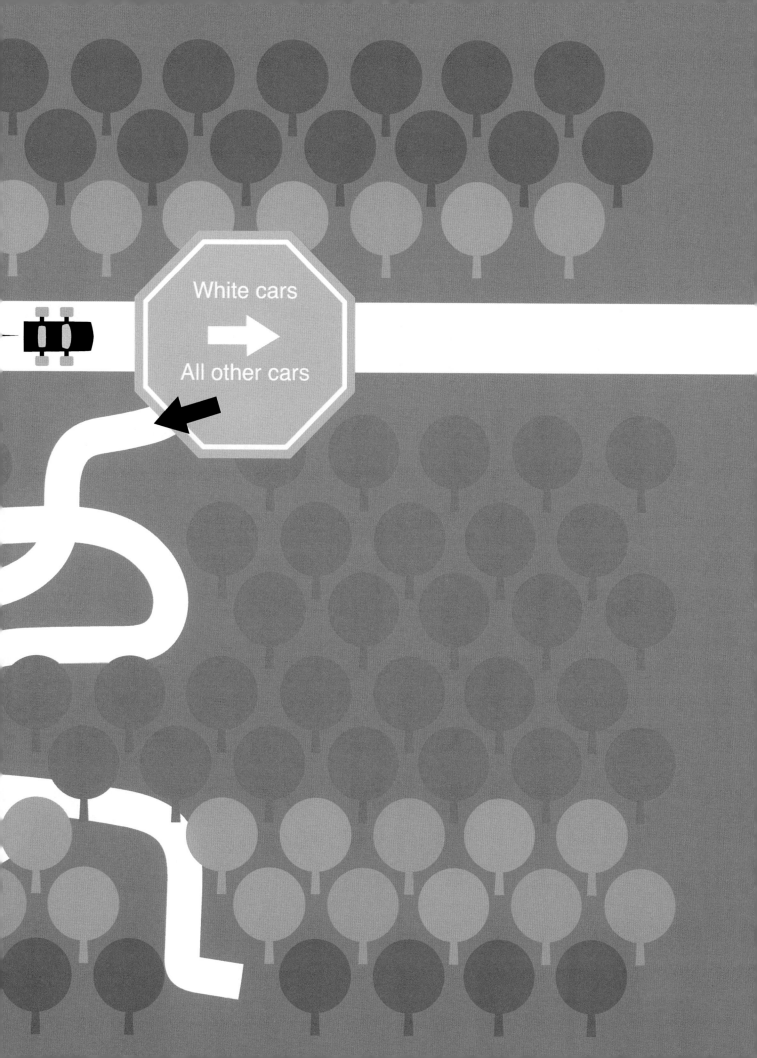

He sped off into the magical forest faster and faster until he realized that he was lost.

"That house wasn't there before! And neither was that owl! Excuse me Mr. Owl, I seem to be lost - could you tell me how to get out of this forest?"

"Why of course! Follow me." The wise friendly owl led chase right through the woods and sent him on his way.

Chase sped around the river as fast as he could and jumped over the finish line. Even though he got lost in the magical forest and could not take the bridge, Chase managed to come in third place. Ace came in second place. Ace was so happy for Chase, and Chase was so happy for Ace. They loved to race and did not care about place.

But back at home, something was bothering Chase. He reminded himself that he just loved racing and that it didn't really matter whether he won or not. But he could not help feeling like he was not as good as the other cars.

Was something wrong with him? Why did he get lost and not Ace? He shrugged it off and decided to train even harder for next year.

Back at Ace's house, Ace was snuggled up in bed smiling. He loved to race and did not care about place, but boy oh boy did it feel good to win a silver medal this year! Ace did not expect to be faster than Chase – in all their practices Chase was always faster than Ace. *"I must be getting much faster"* thought Ace, *"and something must be wrong with Chase"*. He shrugged his shoulders and drifted off to sleep dreaming of next year's race car race.

When the committee heard about Chase winning third place, they were not happy. *"How could a black car have won third place?! This is a disgrace!"* The committee decided to change even more rules to make it easier for the white cars to win the race, just in case!

START

He zipped around the track as the crowds cheered him on.

The next year rolled around and Chase and Ace were ready to race.

Chase started off faster than ever.

He made it up blue mountain in the blink of an eye.

Then he shot through the cornfields in record time.

But at the top of the mountain a race officer stopped him.
"Pull over please, I need to see some identification."
Chase paused for a second, *"Hmm…that's strange"* he
thought, *"none of the white cars seem to be getting stopped?"*
but he did not want to waste any more time. He showed the
officer his identification and continued on his way.

He sped off towards the magical forest. When Chase got to
the forked road in the forest - Mr. Owl was there waiting for
him to show him the way out. The wise friendly owl led Chase
right through the woods and sent him on his way. Chase sped
around the river as fast as he could and jumped over the
finish line. But because the race officer stopped him, Chase
did not get fourth place, or third place, or second place, and
Ace came in first place.

Chase was happy for Ace, but they were both upset about
Chase's race. They loved to race and did not care about
place, but the committee had just announced a new rule.
Cars that did not place this year could no longer race next
year. Next year Chase would not be allowed to race.

Back at home, Chase was devastated. He did not care about place, but he loved to race – what would he do now? Chase could not help feeling like he was not as good as the other cars – something was definitely wrong with him. Why else would he not be allowed to race? That night, Chase cried himself into a long, deep sleep.

Back at Ace's house, Ace was snuggled up in bed. He loved to race and did not care about place, but boy oh boy did it feel good to win a gold medal this year! But something did not feel quite right. He did not understand why Chase did not place – *"he is the fastest car I know!"* thought Ace. Next year would not be the same without his best friend. Chase was the reason that Ace liked to race in the first place! Ace sighed, shrugged his shoulders and drifted off into a long, deep sleep.

START

He zipped around the track as the crowds cheered him on.

Next year rolled around and Chase was at the race to cheer his best friend on.

Ace started off faster than ever.

He made it up blue mountain
in the blink of an eye.

Then he shot through the
cornfields in record time.

Ace was heading for the magical forest when something made him pause. He had seen this sign before but never thought about it too much. This year Ace wanted to know what was down the right path. Ace sped off into the magical forest, faster and faster until he realized that he was lost.

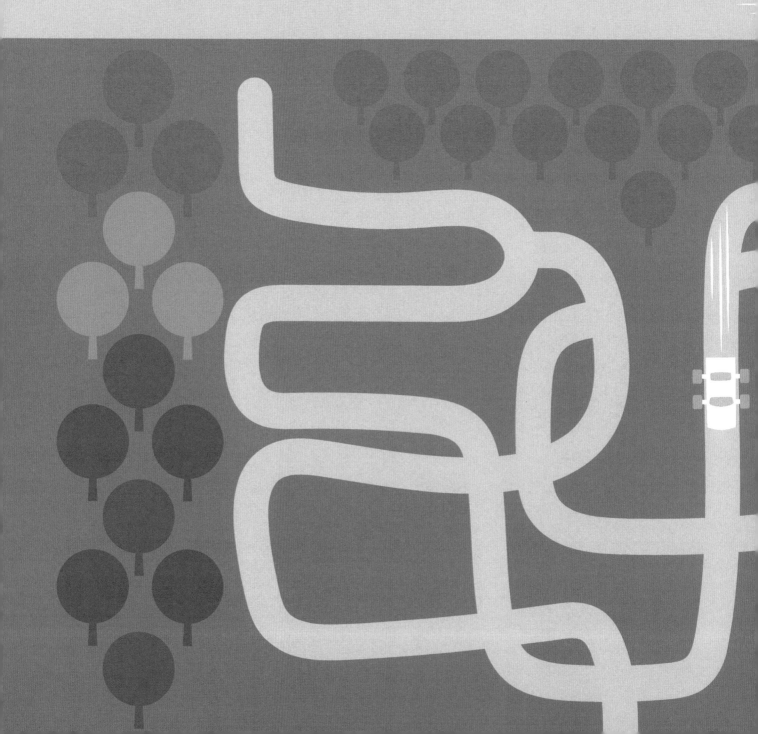

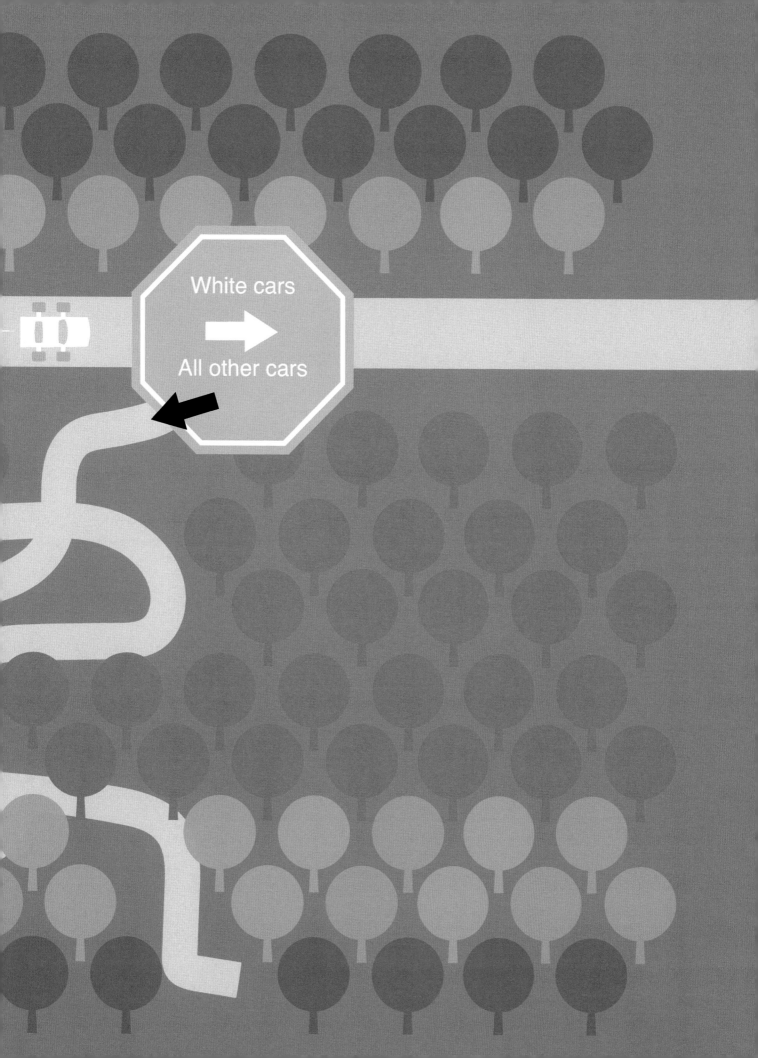

Back at the track, the race officials were starting to get worried. All of the cars had finished the race except for Ace. Where could he be? The race officers looked everywhere but could not find Ace.

The officials called the committee and the committee decided to hold a meeting to figure out the best way to find Ace. *"We need the very fastest race car"* said one. *"the very fastest race car should surely be able to find Ace"* said another. They were all in agreement.

"But the fastest race car is really Chase, even though we did not let him race" added one member. *"If we choose Chase, the world will know that we rigged the race!"*

The committee was reluctant but agreed they MUST save Ace. *"Take down those signs – this is a special case – we must let Chase race at his fastest pace!!"*

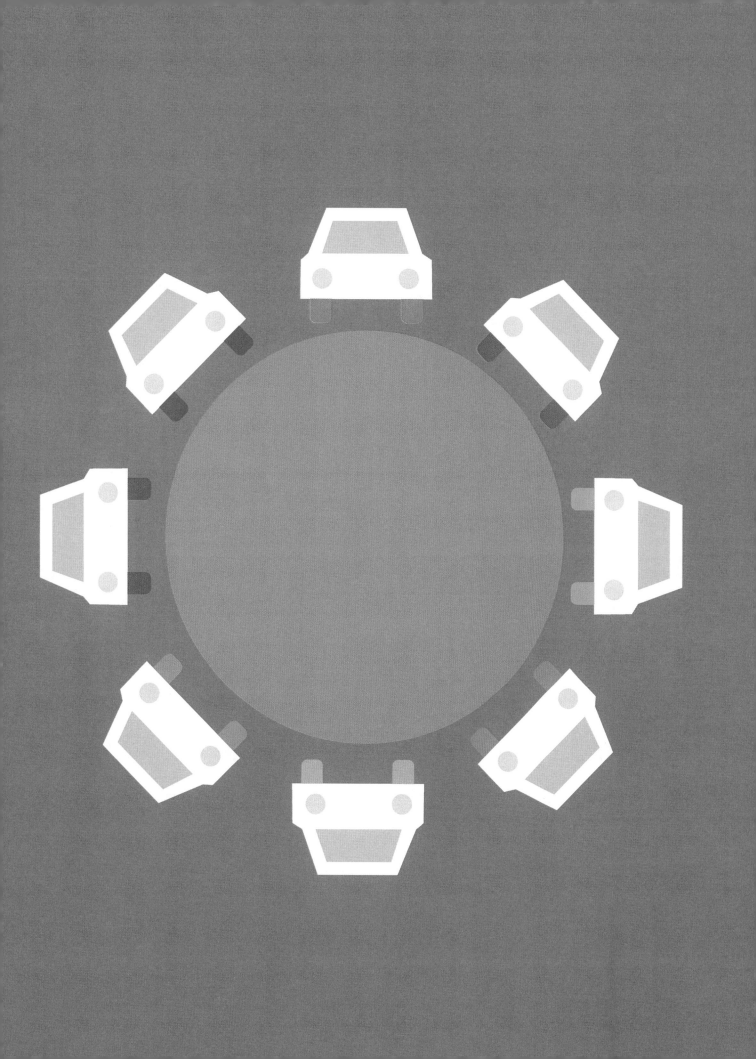

START

He zipped around the track as the crowds cheered him on.

Chase was nervous at first, he was not sure that he was as fast as he once was, but he quickly agreed to save his best friend.

"Here I come, Ace!" said Chase.

He made it up blue mountain in the blink of an eye.

Then he shot through the cornfields in record time.

When he got to the magical forest, Mr. Owl was there waiting to lead him to Ace!

"I'm sorry it took so long for me to realize how much harder it was for you to win this race, Chase" said Ace.

The best friends embraced!

Then, together, Ace and Chase finished the race.

Across the bridge and over the finish line, the friends had finished in record time!!

The committee decided to give Chase the gold medal this year. Ace was so happy for Chase, and Chase was so happy for Ace. Chase did not care about place, but boy oh boy did it feel good to finally win that race!

The end.

TALKING ABOUT RACE CARS WITH KIDS

Think about the story. When reading the story stop at various points to give children a chance to discuss what's happening and what they think will happen next.

Map the characters. Refer back to what you already know about the characters and add new information. Encourage children to make predictions based on this information. For example: *"We know that Chase is a black car and that the organizers of the race want a white car to win. What do you think they might do to make sure he does not win? Is that fair?"*

Pay attention to non-verbal cues. Amplify subtle messages to call attention to unnoticed communicative behavior such as tone of voice, body language or facial expressions. This is especially important when reading with more than one child. For example, if all of the children are laughing but one child looks upset and the other children have not noticed, say something like, "Johnny is not laughing" and wait for responses from the other children. Continually scanning for non-verbal cues is one way to elevate the voices of children with less dominant opinions that may find it hard to express a view that is different from the majority.

Reach for feelings. Have children consider what the characters in the book might be feeling as they read the story. *"Can you imagine what Chase must be feeling in this moment?"* *"Has anyone else ever felt a little bit like what Chase is feeling right now?"*

Invite full participation. When discussing difficult topics such as race, some children may tend to shut down. Often white children may become silent because they feel they have nothing to add to the conversation. Children of color that make up a minority of the group may feel uncomfortable expressing their opinion, especially when they are noticing aspects of the story that are not obvious to their white peers. Search for new voices by pointing out what you are observing. *"Only the students of color have shared. Would any of the white students like to say something?"* *"What makes it difficult to talk about this story?"* *"Only the boys are talking, I would love to hear from some of the girls as well."* However, be careful not to single out students of color or rely on them to be the 'expert' on all things related to race.

DISCUSSION QUESTIONS FOR RACE CARS

What color cars usually win the race?

What do you think it was like for Chase to be the first black car to win the race?

What do you think some other reactions to him winning might have been?

Why do you think the race committee was so upset that Chase won the race?

When Chase is getting ready to cross the bridge he notices a sign "Bridge is for white cars only." What do you think it felt like for Chase to see that sign? What do you think it felt like for Ace to see that sign? Is that sign fair, or unfair? Why?

What is the difference between Chase's and Ace's reactions to the race?

Ace does not seem to notice all of the extra barriers Chase has to go through to finish the race. Why do you think he might not realize what Chase is going through? Why does he think he is winning the race, and not Chase? Why is he really winning the race?

Can you think of any real life situations where the rules are different for one group versus another group? Is this fair or unfair? (*Here, it can be useful to start with an easier concept for them to grasp such as boys vs. girls, children vs. adults, etc. They may need to be prompted - encourage them to think about white people vs. people of color, disabled people, LGBTQ, etc.*)

In this book, the white cars get special privileges that the black cars do not. **Privilege** *is a special advantage or immunity or benefit not enjoyed by all. Even though Ace did not ask for those privileges, he is still benefitting from them simply by being a white car. The same is true for people as well.*

White privilege *provides white people with privileges that they do not earn and that people of color do not enjoy. White privilege is not something that white people necessarily do, create or enjoy on purpose, but it is something that they all benefit from.*

Can you think of some advantages that people get because they are white?
You can give some examples to start off the discussion:

When you cut your finger and go to the school or office's first aid kit, do the "flesh-colored" band-aids match your skin tone?

When you go to the store to buy dolls, is it easy to find dolls that look like you?"

Made in the USA
Columbia, SC
23 August 2020